"What am I to do with you?" Azzon snapped.

Zantor was still shuffling around the room, poking his head into this and that, snuffling and sniffling. Now there came a sudden crash and they all jumped.

"*Zatz!*" shouted Azzon. "Look what your beast has done!"

Zantor had upset a shelf high up on the wall. Bottles, jugs, and beakers tumbled to the floor.

"Sorry!" cried Darek. "He didn't mean anything. He was probably just looking for something to eat."

"Dratted dragon!" Azzon shouted. "Those are my potions!" He strode across the room and knelt beside Zantor, trying to salvage what he could. Darek ran over to try to help. Then suddenly he stopped in his tracks. Zantor was shrinking!

"Zantor!" he cried. "What's happening?"

Dragon Trouble

Jackie French Koller

Illustrated by Judith Mitchell

THIS BOOK WAS CHOSEN BY:

Anabel ♡

AT A S.K. FAUST SCHOOL
R.I.F. BOOK FAIR

A
MINSTREL® BOOK

Published by POCKET BOOKS
New York   London   Toronto   Sydney   Tokyo   Singapore

This book is a work of fiction. Names, characters, places and incidents are products of the author's imagination or are used fictitiously. Any resemblance to actual events or locales or persons living or dead is entirely coincidental.

A MINSTREL PAPERBACK *Original*

 A Minstrel Book published by
POCKET BOOKS, a division of Simon & Schuster Inc.
1230 Avenue of the Americas, New York, NY 10020

ISBN: 0-671-01399-8

First Minstrel Books printing November 1997

10 9 8 7 6 5 4 3 2 1

A MINSTREL BOOK and colophon are registered trademarks of Simon & Schuster Inc.

Cover art by Judith Mitchell

Printed in the U.S.A.

Prologue

Legend has it that the people of Zoriac originally came from a green valley called Zor, beyond the dreaded Black Mountains, and that fierce men known as Kradens drove them out and renamed the valley Krad. Some Zorians believe the legends. Others say that Zor was a mythical place and the great, hairy-faced Kradens are nothing but fairy tale creatures. No one knows for sure, because no one has ever ventured into the Black Mountains and returned to tell of it, until now.

When a runaway wagon carried Darek's best

friend, Pola, and four baby Blue dragons into the Black Mountains, Darek and Rowena, daughter of the Chief Elder, felt responsible. It was their selfishness that had led to the accident. Together, they defied the laws of Zoriac and went after their friends. Now the three children are back safely and they have rescued three of the four Blue dragons, including Darek's beloved dragon, Zantor. But all is not well. It seems that their fathers and Darek's brother, Clep, went into the mountains after them, and have not returned. The children are desperate to get their loved ones back, but they can't even remember how *they* got back. Their memories were erased in Krad. Zantor, who can send mind messages to Darek and Rowena, is helping them piece the past together, but it is slow going. Will they remember in time to save their fathers? Or is it already too late?

1

Darek sat on the paddock fence, staring. Out in the fields Zantor and the two female dragons, Drizba and Typra, grazed peacefully. The zorgrass obviously agreed with them. They had grown tremendously in the few weeks since Darek had been back at home. Zantor still insisted on sleeping by Darek's bed each night. But that couldn't go on much longer. Zantor could barely squeeze through the door anymore!

Little by little, Darek was trying to piece together what had happened to him since Zantor

came into his life. He and his friends Pola and
Rowena had been to Krad and back. He knew
that much. But someone, or something, had taken
away their memories while they were there. Not

just their memories of Krad, but their memories of several anums before, too. Darek's mother had been doing her best to fill in those anums for him.

Zantor was helping, too. He was able to send Darek and his friend Rowena mind pictures of things he had heard and seen. These mind messages were giving them back memories of Krad. Darek hadn't shared these memories with his mother yet because he didn't want to worry her. They were too awful to share—scenes of a bleak, smoke-shrouded land, where Zorians were slaves, and fierce, hairy Kradens ruled. Darek swallowed hard. His father and brother were still in Krad somewhere, and Pola's and Rowena's fathers, too. That is—if any of them were still alive.

Darek heard a shout and turned to see Pola and Rowena coming up the road.

"How's he doing?" asked Rowena. She hopped up on the fence and nodded toward the scar on Zantor's neck. Zantor and Darek had both been wounded by arrows in their escape from Krad.

"Good as new," said Darek. "Look at him."

The three friends watched as Zantor charged the other two dragons in a play battle. Drizba and Typra reared and screamed in mock terror. Darek, Pola, and Rowena laughed.

"How about you?" Pola asked then. "How's the leg coming along?"

Darek rubbed his thigh. "A little stiff still, but nothing I can't handle. Any further word on our punishment?"

"No." Rowena bit her lip. There was a law in Zoriac that anyone caught venturing into the Black Mountains was to be put to death. Pola did not need to worry. He had been carried into the mountains by accident. But Darek and Rowena had gone after him willingly. Under Zorian law, when a child under twelve broke the law, the child's father was made to suffer the punishment, even if that father was Chief Elder, like Rowena's father. But Darek's father and the Chief Elder were gone, along with Pola's father and Darek's brother. They had gone into the Black Mountains,

6

too, to search for the children. And they had not returned.

"It's all so confusing," Rowena went on. "Mother says the elders can't decide what to do. I worry what will happen when our fathers get back, though. Zarnak, the acting chief, seems very fond of that crown on his head. I think he will be all too glad of a reason to put my father to death."

Pola shook his head firmly. "Your father has too many friends on the Council," he said to Rowena. "And Darek, your father is one of the most respected men in the village. Don't worry about that old law. It was only made to scare Zorians away from the Black Mountains for their own safety."

"That's not quite true," said Rowena. "It was also meant to prevent Zorians from going over the mountains and provoking the Kradens, *if* they in fact existed."

"Thrummm, thrummm, thrummm!" The young dragons had noticed the children and came loping

over. They stuck their heads over the fence to be petted.

"Here," Darek said, pulling some sugar cubes from his jerkin pocket. He handed a few to Pola and Rowena. "Zantor reminded me yesterday that he loves these."

The three children held out the cubes and, *thwippp, thwippp, thwippp!* The dragons gobbled them eagerly.

"Have you gotten any more mind messages from Zantor?" Rowena asked Darek as they watched the dragons munch.

"Shush!" Darek glanced back toward the house. "I don't think my mother, or anyone else, should know what we've found out about Krad until we can figure a way to get our fathers back."

"Why?" asked Rowena.

"Because I don't trust Zarnak. As far as I'm concerned, the less he knows, the better."

Rowena and Pola nodded their agreement.

"The last memory I can get from Zantor," Darek went on, "is when the arrow struck my leg.

But . . . how did we get home? We made it through the mists *somehow*."

Pola and Rowena nodded again. They had learned from Zantor's mind messages that the mists in the Black Mountains were poisonous. The poison was deadly to Kradens, and robbed Zorians of their minds.

"We've *got* to find out how we did it," said Darek.

"Why?" asked Pola. "What are you planning?"

Darek glanced toward the house and then lowered his voice. "I'm going back," he said.

A wry smile slowly curled Pola's lips. "When do we leave?" he asked.

"I didn't say *we*," said Darek. "I said *me*. I'm already in trouble. You're not."

Pola bristled. "Oh, right," he said, "like I'd ever let you go alone. My father's over there, too, don't forget."

"And mine!" Rowena put in.

Both boys turned to look at her. "You're not

suggesting we take *you* back there?" said Darek. "It's too dangerous!"

Rowena crossed her arms over her chest and narrowed her eyes. "Nobody *takes* me anywhere," she said. "I go where I *please*. And *if* I please to go with you, I *will*. Just like I did last time."

"*Rrronk!*" came a sudden cry. The young dragons had finished the sugar cubes and gone back to their games. Apparently Zantor had started playing a little too rough, knocking Drizba down. As Darek, Pola, and Rowena watched, Drizba got to her feet, threw back her head, and spread her wings.

"*Grrrawwk!*" she screamed in a *very* convincing imitation of an angry, full-grown Blue.

"*Rrronk, rrronk!*" cried Zantor. He barreled across the field, leapt the fence in a single bound, and dove for cover behind Darek.

"Wow," said Darek, "she's pretty impressive when she gets mad. I thought for a minute she was going to breathe fire."

"Who?" asked Pola, grinning widely, "Drizba, or Rowena?"

2

_____

"Mother?" Darek called.

"Up here," Alayah answered.

Darek climbed the narrow, winding staircase to the garret.

"Rrronk," cried Zantor. Darek looked back and saw him wedged in the doorway. The garret stairs were too narrow for him.

"Silly dragon," said Darek. He went back down and pushed Zantor free. "Just wait here," he said. "I'll only be a moment." Zantor's head sagged. He rested his chin on one of the lower steps and watched sadly as Darek climbed up, out of his reach.

Alayah was just closing an old chest as Darek entered the garret. She dabbed quickly at her eyes with her apron.

"What are you doing?" Darek asked.

"Nothing," she said, "just . . ." Her voice trailed off.

Darek walked over and crouched down beside her. "What's in here?" he asked. Before his mother could answer, he lifted the lid and looked in. The chest was full of yellowed letters and baby clothes. Some of his father's old uniforms, medals, and archery trophies were there, too.

"Just memories," Darek's mother said softly.

Darek lifted out one of the trophies and sat with it on his lap. He thought of the days when he and Clep were small. Often, in the evenings, after supper, his father would set a target up beyond the barn and let them practice with his great bow. At first Darek had been too small even to bend the string, but his father would twine his fingers through Darek's and help him pull.

"You did it!" Clep would cry when the arrow found its mark. Then Darek would feel proud, even though he knew he couldn't have done it without his father.

Tears sprang to Darek's eyes. How he missed his father and brother. Sadly, he replaced the trophy in the chest. He was about to close it again when he noticed something in the corner. It looked like a mask of some sort.

"What's this?" he asked, lifting the object out.

"Oh, that old thing," his mother said, wrinkling her nose. "That was your great-grandfather's battle mask."

"Battle mask?" Darek repeated. "I never heard of a battle mask."

"The men haven't used them since the Red Fangs disappeared," Alayah explained.

Darek's ears perked up. There were still Red Fangs in Krad—hundreds of them! It was their breath that poisoned the mists in the mountains.

"Why did the men wear masks to fight the Red Fangs?" he asked.

"Something about their breath," his mother replied. "It was poisonous, I think."

Darek's heart thumped quickly as he turned the strange mask over in his hand. "And the masks filtered the poison out?" he asked.

"I believe so." His mother nodded.

Darek couldn't believe his ears. This was it! This was his answer! Now he could go back to Krad.

"Are there any more of these?" he asked.

"A few perhaps, in the archives in Elder Hall. Why?"

When Darek didn't answer right away a cloud of fear darkened Alayah's eyes. Her hand went to her chest.

"What are you thinking?" she asked worriedly.

Darek looked at her. He couldn't lie to her— couldn't leave her again without explanation.

"These masks make it possible for me to go after Father and Clep," he said.

A small cry escaped Alayah's lips and tears filled her eyes again. "Oh, I was afraid of this," she said softly.

"I must go," Darek said gently. "Please . . . don't try to stop me."

His mother wiped her tears and put her arms around him. "I would try, if I could," she said with a sigh, "but I know I can't. Trying to stop you from following your heart is like trying to stop a river from flowing. You'll only boil and churn until you find another way to burst out and rush away."

Darek looked up into his mother's eyes. He'd never known she was so wise, and brave. "Thank you for understanding," he said.

"Thank *you* for giving me a chance to say good-bye this time," she answered.

3

Darek, Pola, and Rowena crouched in the bushes below Elder Hall. The building was tall and imposing. Fierce stone dragon heads glared down at them from the rooftop. A pair of armed guards flanked the door.

"How are we supposed to get past them?" Darek whispered.

"Maybe there's another way in," said Pola.

Rowena shook her head. "The back door is kept chained and barred," she said. "There's only one way in and you're looking at it."

"Then we need a decoy," said Darek. He looked at Rowena.

She frowned. "Why me?" she asked. "Why can't one of you be the decoy?"

"Because they all know you," said Darek. "Your father's Chief Elder."

"Which is why Zarnak hates me," Rowena reminded him. "He'd love another chance to humiliate me and my family."

"But the guards are still loyal to your father," said Darek. "They'll help you. You know they will."

Rowena looked at Darek doubtfully. "What do you want me to do?" she asked.

"I don't know. Pretend you're hurt or something."

Rowena huffed. "I don't like it," she said. "Why do I have to be the damsel in distress while you get to have all the fun?"

Darek snorted. "Fun?" he said. "Sneaking around in the dungeons of that creepy old hall? I'd be happy to trade places, but be serious. If

Pola or I go up there and fall on our faces in front of those guys they'll just laugh their heads off."

Rowena rolled her eyes. "All right, I'll do it," she said. "But I won't like it."

"Nobody's asking you to like it," said Darek. "Just get going, okay? Time's wasting."

Rowena slipped around to the side of the building and back down the hillside. Darek and Pola crept farther up the bank. They waited, hidden, just below the front steps.

"Lady Rowena!" they heard one of the guards shout after a while.

"Good morning," they heard Rowena call from below. Then a cry. "Aaagh!"

Darek winked at Pola. "Very convincing," he whispered.

"Milady!" both guards cried at once. They dropped their lances and hurried down the stairs.

Darek and Pola crept out of the bushes and up the steps, keeping deep in the shadows.

"Oww, oww, oooh," they heard Rowena moan.

20

They could see her writing on the ground with both guards bent over her.

"Hurry," said Darek as he pushed one of the great doors open. Both boys slipped inside, scurried for a dark corner, and stopped to catch their breath.

There was no one in sight. They listened for voices or footsteps, but there were none. Elder Hall was silent and forbidding, lit only by flickering torchlight. Darek and Pola stared in awe. Neither had ever been inside before. They were in a small entry hall. An arched doorway beyond led into the Council Room. Darek and Pola crept forward to have a better look.

"Wow," whispered Darek. Adorning the walls were dragon skins of all colors. They hung at angles as if diving out of the sky. Their tails curled up and across the great, high ceiling. Their glassy eyes were fixed on the Council Table, which stretched the length of the room. Their mouths gaped open, fangs barred, in imitation of battle screams. On an elevated platform at the far end of the room stood the Chief Elder's throne. It was carved in the shape of a sitting dragon. The head was real—it was the stuffed head of a Great Blue.

Darek shuddered. "I'm glad we didn't bring Zantor," he said.

Pola nodded. "Yeah. Let's get this over with. This place gives me the creeps."

Darek looked around. To one side of the front doors a stairway wound down into darkness.

"Grab a torch and follow me," he said.

He and Pola grabbed the two closest torches and started down. The stairs grew steeper and narrower as they went. At the bottom was a long, narrow passageway with doors opening off each side.

"Where do we start?" asked Pola. "We don't have much time. Those guards aren't going to listen to Rowena whine forever."

Darek pushed a door open and thrust his torch inside. "Lord E . . . !" he cried.

"What is it?" asked Pola, trying to peek around him.

"I think it's an old torture chamber of some kind," Darek whispered. "Look."

He stood to one side and Pola peeked in. The room was so thick with cobwebs it was hard to see. There were spikes sticking everywhere out of the walls and up from the floor. Chains dangled from ceiling and walls.

"Lord Eternal," whispered Pola. "There's no place to sit or lie down without being pierced!"

"And we thought the Kradens were cruel," said Darek. "Looks like Zorians can be pretty cruel, too."

Suddenly there was a sound overhead. It sounded like footsteps. Darek and Pola froze. A minute went by, then two. The sound didn't come again.

"Our imaginations must be playing tricks on us," said Darek. "Come on. Let's find those masks and get out of here."

They peeked into a number of other chambers and cells, until at last they came to a room filled with dusty trunks and cupboards.

"This looks like the archives," Darek whispered. "Hurry."

They put their torches into holders on the walls and started tearing open drawers and throwing back the lids of trunks. They found stacks of old books and scrolls, chests full of rusted armor and old weapons.

"Here they are!" Pola cried at last.

Darek ran over and looked down. In the chest at Pola's feet lay a mound of battle masks.

"Great!" cried Darek. He grabbed several of the masks and shoved them inside his shirt. Pola did the same.

"That should do it," said Darek. "Let's go."

They turned toward the door, but then froze in their tracks. Leaning against the door frame, arms folded over his chest, was Zarnak!

"Interested in history, are you, boys?" he asked wryly.

4

Darek, Pola, and Rowena waited off to one side. Their mothers stood before Zarnak. The battle masks lay in a heap on the Council table.

"Why were your children in the archives?" Zarnak demanded. "What use have they for these masks?"

Rowena's mother, the Grand Dame, shrugged. "They are children," she said.

"Yes," Pola's mother chimed in. "You know how curious children are. I'll wager you tried to sneak into Elder Hall yourself as a boy."

Zarnak did not look amused. He turned toward Darek and Pola.

"What use have you for these masks?" he repeated.

"We were going play Dragon Quest with them," said Darek.

"Yes," agreed Pola. "It was just a game."

Zarnak's eyes narrowed.

"A game, eh?" he said. "A game like . . . trying to rescue your fathers?"

Darek's heart thumped. "N-no," he stammered.

"Would that they *could* rescue their fathers," the Grand Dame interrupted angrily. "But look at them. They are but children. It is you, Zarnak, who should be about the business of rescuing their fathers."

Zarnak shifted uncomfortably in his seat. "You know the Council voted against a rescue," he said. "We still don't know what dangers lie beyond the Black Mountains. If these children had not disobeyed the law in the first place their fathers would not be in trouble. Your husband, Grand

Dame, would not wish me to place the whole village at risk for his sake."

The Grand Dame's eyes flashed. "You may fool others with that lie, Zarnak," she said. "But you don't fool me. I know who swayed the Council against a rescue, and I can well see how fond you've grown of that throne."

Zarnak and the Grand Dame stared at each other in stony silence for a long moment, then he motioned to the guards. "Escort these women and children to the door!" he shouted.

As Pola, Rowena, and Darek turned to go, Zarnak pointed a sharp finger at them. "Be warned," he boomed. "Children or not, I will have you in the stocks the next time I catch you sneaking about!"

5

After supper, Darek's mother went out on an errand. Darek, Pola, and Rowena sat beside the hearth. Zantor, who now filled half the room, sprawled behind them, with his neck over Darek's shoulder and his head in Rowena's lap.

"We've *got* to find a way to go back," said Rowena. She looked down into Zantor's eyes. "Tell us more, Zantor," she said. "We must know how we got out of Krad."

Darek reached up on the mantel and took down the arrow that he had pulled from Zantor's neck.

He placed the point over the wound in his leg and made a motion like he was pulling it out. "Who took the arrow out of my leg, Zantor?" he asked. "Do you remember anything?"

The young dragon stared at the arrow. A misty image began to take shape in Darek's mind. "I'm getting something!" said Rowena.

"Shush!" said Darek. "Me, too." In his head he saw his own body lying crumpled on the rocky soil of the Black Mountains. Bent little creatures crowded around him. One of them grasped the arrow shaft and pulled it free. Then the image started to fade.

"What else, Zantor?" asked Darek. "Who are those creatures? Where did they take me?"

But Zantor's great, green eyes only stared at him blankly.

"What did he show you?" asked Pola.

"The creatures who rescued me," said Darek. "But I have no idea who or what they are."

"If only we could find them," said Rowena. "If

they helped us, maybe they helped our fathers and Clep, too."

"Not much chance of finding them without the masks," said Darek quietly.

Suddenly the door opened and Darek's mother rushed in. With her was the Grand Dame herself.

"Mother!" cried Rowena in surprise. She, Darek, and Pola jumped to their feet.

"Hurry," whispered the Grand Dame, motioning to someone still outside. A guard entered, bearing a chest.

"What the . . . ?" said Darek.

"Put them there," the Grand Dame commanded, pointing to the kitchen table. "Then be gone. You have seen nothing and heard nothing. Do you understand?"

The guard nodded. He lowered the chest to the table, and emptied its contents.

"The masks!" cried Darek.

The guard slipped silently back out into the night. The Grand Dame closed the door after him. Then she turned and smiled.

"My husband has many friends," she said. Then she looked at Rowena. "Why did you not seek my help at the outset?" she asked.

"I . . . I did not think you would be willing," said Rowena.

The Grand Dame came forward and gently smoothed her daughter's hair. She put a hand on Rowena's shoulder and gazed proudly but sadly into her eyes. "Did you think," she said gently, "that Alayah was the only mother capable of understanding the destiny of her child?"

Zantor, Drizba, and Typra were saddled and ready to go. The young dragons were in high spirits. They seemed eager for the adventure, but Darek, Pola, and Rowena were solemn. Their mothers stood beside them in the early morning chill.

"Is it cold in Krad?" Darek's mother asked. "Perhaps you should bring cloaks."

"Yes, and rain hoods," said the Grand Dame. "Wait a bit. I'll run back and get them." She turned and took a step but Rowena called her back. Rowena, Pola, and Darek exchanged glances. They knew their mothers were raising these small worries to keep from voicing the larger ones. And to forestall the leavetaking.

"We have to go," Darek told the women quietly. "The longer we wait, the greater the chance the elders will discover us."

33

The three mothers nodded bravely, but all of them blinked back tears.

"Take care," Alayah whispered. She stepped forward and kissed Darek good-bye. Then she patted Zantor's neck. "Watch over him, my friend," she pleaded softly. Zantor tossed his head regally as if to say, "Fear not."

Darek climbed into the saddle and fitted his mask over his face. "Ready?" he called to Pola and Rowena. His voice, through the mask, had a muffled, metallic sound.

Pola and Rowena kissed their mothers good-bye, then mounted their dragons and put on their masks. In their saddlebags were the remaining masks. There were just enough for the fathers and Clep, and one spare. The others had been too old and rotted to be of use.

"Ready," Pola and Rowena cried.

"Push off!" Darek commanded.

Zantor crouched down, unfurled his wings, and then sprang upward! With a mighty downward

sweep of wings, they were airborne. Darek felt a rush of exhilaration.

"We'll be back!" he cried over his shoulder. Their mothers, waving below, grew smaller as the ground fell away. "And Clep and our fathers will be with us!" Darek promised.

6

Thick, damp smoke swirled around them. But thanks to the masks, Darek, Pola, and Rowena could not smell the foul breath of the Black Mountains. Below them the landscape was barren and forbidding. There were rocks and stumps and scrubby bushes. Everything was black and charred, as if it had been swept by a forest fire.

Zantor seemed to know where he was going. He and the other dragons were flying strongly. They seemed to have no problem carrying riders anymore.

"Stay close," Darek called to Pola and Rowena as the smog thickened. They were in the heart of the mountains now. Darek was keeping a sharp eye out for movement below. They were looking for the creatures that Darek had seen in Zantor's last mind message.

"There!" cried Rowena. She pointed to a clearing. Out of the corner of his eye, Darek saw a number of small shapes scurry into the scrub.

"Down!" he commanded.

The three dragons tipped their wings and circled down. Darek, Pola, and Rowena dismounted. The clearing was empty, but there were little sharp-toed footprints everywhere.

"Hello!" Darek cried. "Don't be afraid. We come in peace."

Pola gave a hollow-sounding laugh. "If they're watching," he said, "they're bound to be frightened. These masks would scare anyone."

"You're right," said Darek. "I'll take mine off, just for a minute." He pulled his mask off and pushed back his hair. To his amazement he heard murmurs of surprise and delight all around him.

"It be him!" the creatures were calling to one another. "Dragon Boy be back!" A number of small, gray-scaled creatures emerged from the underbrush. One of them came forward. "Welcome, me friend!" he said with a wide, yellow-toothed grin.

"Who are you?" asked Darek. Then he looked around at the other creatures and added, "*What* are you?"

"Me, Zooba," said the one who had stepped forward. "Me be Dragon Boy's friend. Ye fix me leg. Me fix ye leg." Zooba pointed to a dark scar on his thigh. Then he swept his hand toward his friends. "We be Zynots. Remember ye now?"

"My name is not Dragon Boy. It's Darek," Darek told the little creature. "And these are my friends, Pola and Rowena. I'm afraid we don't remember much about our last visit."

"Ahhh." Zooba made a high, twittering sound

that Darek guessed to be laughter. "That be because of potion. Azzon took memories."

"Azzon?" said Darek. "Who's Azzon?"

"Azzon King of Krad," said Zooba. He put out a small, lizardlike hand. "Take you there."

"No, no!" said Darek quickly. "We don't want to go to Krad. Not yet anyway."

"Azzon not in Krad," said Zooba. "Azzon here."

"Here?" repeated Darek. This concerned him. He had thought they would be safe from the Kradens as long as they stayed in the mountains.

"Yes," said Zooba. "Come."

The clearing was full of Zynots now, all murmuring together and staring at the newcomers. Smaller ones, children probably, climbed all over Zantor and the other two dragons, petting them and chattering excitedly.

Darek looked up into Zantor's eyes. "You all right?" he asked as a little Zynot crawled out on the dragon's nose.

"Thrummm," sang Zantor. Apparently he was fond of these creatures.

"Come," Zooba insisted, grabbing Darek's hand and tugging.

Darek gave a cough and replaced his mask. "No," he said again. "You don't understand. Kradens are our enemies. They'll hurt us."

"Azzon no hurt," said Zooba. "Azzon help."

7

Zooba led them deep under the mountains, through a steep, winding tunnel. Zantor, Drizba, and Typra and a gaggle of giggling zynots followed.

At last Zooba stopped. "Don't need masks now," he said. "Safe for ye here."

It was true. The dragonsbreath didn't seem to reach this far underground. Darek, Pola, and Rowena removed their masks and put them in their saddlebags. Zooba gave a small cough. "Go ye alone, now," he said. "Follow tunnel."

Darek stroked Zantor's neck. "The tunnel is getting narrow," he said. "You dragons stay here and play with your new little friends. We won't be long."

"*Rrronk,*" cried Zantor softly.

Darek smiled. "Don't worry," he said. "We'll be okay."

Darek, Pola, and Rowena went on alone. At last the tunnel widened into a cavern and they came to a great door.

"Guess this is it," whispered Darek.

"Guess so," said Pola.

Rowena nodded.

"Guess we should knock," said Darek.

"Guess so," said Pola.

Rowena nodded.

Darek stood staring at the great knocker.

"Well?" said Pola.

"Well what?" whispered Darek.

"Well, are you going to knock?"

Darek frowned. "Why do I have to do everything? Why don't you knock?"

"Me?" Pola protested. "What are you talking about? I do as much as you . . ."

"Oh, for pity's sake," snapped Rowena. Before either boy could say another word she grabbed the great knocker and slammed it down.

"KABOOM . . . BOOM . . . BOOM . . . BOOM!" The sound bounced around the cavern and echoed far back into the tunnel.

Instantly the door flew open and a fierce, hairy face stared down at them. For a moment, the tall, graying man seemed taken aback. Then his brows crashed into a deep V.

"You!" he bellowed. "I thought I had seen the last of you!"

Darek, Pola, and Rowena huddled together.

"You . . . you know us?" Darek stammered.

"Know you? Who do you think nursed you back to health and took you home?"

"You?" Darek's eyes widened in surprise. "But . . . the Zynots said you were the King of Krad."

"The *exiled* King of Krad," Azzon boomed. "Remember?"

44

Darek swallowed hard. "We remember very little," he said.

This seemed to calm Azzon. He stared at them,
pulling thoughtfully at his beard. "So, the potion
did work," he said after a time. "But, then, how
came you back again?"

Darek swallowed hard. He didn't know if he

should trust this man. But the Zynots said he would help, and it seemed he had helped before . . .

"*How?*" Azzon bellowed. "Tell me before I feed you to the Red Fangs!"

Darek jumped. "The dragon showed us," he said.

"Dragon?" Azzon's eyes narrowed. "What dragon?"

Suddenly there was a heavy rumble of footsteps. Then a commotion of huffing and puffing, scratching and scraping, shrieking and giggling. And then into the cavern thundered Zantor, a dozen little Zynots still clinging to his back.

A smile tugged at Darek's lips. Zantor must have heard the *boom* of the knocker and gotten worried. "*That* dragon," he said.

Zantor had a wild look in his eyes, but when he saw Darek he grew calm. He loped over, then *thwippp!* Out flicked his tongue, planting a kiss on Darek's cheek.

Azzon stared openmouthed at the gentle blue

46

giant. Then he shook his head, and his anger seemed to melt away. "Now I've seen everything," he said.

The Zynot children twittered merrily.

"All right," said Azzon in a kindly voice. "Home with you now before you take ill." He plucked the Zynots off Zantor one by one. Giggling and tumbling over each other, they scurried back up the tunnel.

Now it was Darek, Pola, and Rowena who stared in wonder. Could this kindly old man truly be the King of Krad? Kradens were supposed to be fierce and cruel.

Azzon looked after the Zynots wistfully. "Would that they *could* stay and play," he said softly, almost to himself.

"Why can't they?" asked Darek.

"Their bodies have adapted to the dragons-breath," said Azzon. "It's all they can breathe now."

"What did they breathe before?" Pola asked.

"The same thing you breathe," said Azzon. "In the Long Ago they were Zorians, like you."

Darek, Pola and Rowena gaped at Azzon.

"We're related to *them?*" asked Rowena.

"Yes," said Azzon, "but enough about Zynots. Why are you here?"

"Our fathers are somewhere in Krad," said Darek. "And my brother, too. We've come to rescue them."

"Ahhh." Humor glittered in Azzon's eyes. "And how do you propose to do that?"

"We're not sure," said Darek. "We thought you might help us."

"I?" Azzon chuckled. "Why would I turn against my own sons and help you?"

"Your sons?" Rowena repeated.

"Yes." Azzon sighed. "My sons rule Krad now, Zahr here in the north, and Rebbe in the south. But I've told you all this before. Come. For all the good the memory potion has done, I might as well give you the antidote. But first you must give me your word that you will never do anything to bring harm to my sons."

Darek, Pola, and Rowena glanced at one another in surprise. How could *they* possibly harm Azzon's sons?

"Agreed?" Azzon asked.

Darek shrugged. "Of course. You have my word."

"Mine too. And mine," added Pola and Rowena. Then the three followed Azzon into a large, torchlit cave. Zantor squeezed through the door right behind them.

"Aack, aack," came a small cough.

Darek looked up to see a small Zynot still perched, like a crown, on the top of Zantor's head.

"Mizzle!" cried Azzon. "Down from there this minute!"

Mizzle slid down Zantor's back and off his tail, twittering wildly.

"Out of here. Now!" shouted Azzon. He swatted playfully at the child's rear as it scurried out the door.

8

Azzon's antidote worked like magic. For the first time in months, Darek felt himself again. There were no empty gaps anymore. No more questions unanswered. He remembered all about Azzon now. How his two sons had turned against each other, and then against him. How Azzon had nearly died, fleeing into the Black Mountains. How the Zynots had rescued him and brought him to this cave, deep underground.

"This is wonderful!" cried Rowena. "I remember everything!"

"I, too," Pola agreed.

"Thank you, Azzon," said Darek. "We are grateful."

Azzon nodded solemnly. "Just remember your promise," he said. Then he filled his pipe and sank into a chair. He motioned to Darek, Pola, and Rowena to be seated as well. Then he lit his pipe and puffed quietly.

Zantor was snuffling around the room, exploring. Darek looked around, too. It was a great, dark cave, lit by torches. But it was quite richly furnished. How did Azzon come by such things here, underground? he wondered. Azzon caught his eye and seemed to read his mind.

"You like my decor?" he asked with a smile.

"Yes," said Darek, "it's . . ."

"Surprising," Rowena put in.

Azzon chuckled. "The Zynots are not so dull-witted as one might think," he said. "Every year, about this time, when the days grow warm and the ground is still cold, the dragonsbreath settles low into the valley at night, like fog. The Kradens and their Zorian slaves must stay inside with doors and shutters sealed tight. But the Zynots are free, as long as there is no wind or rain, to come down from their mountains. They scamper about, shrieking and moaning. They pummel the doors and rattle the shutters. It's really quite convincing."

"You mean . . . the Kradens think they are spirits?" said Pola.

"Yes." Azzon laughed. "I was humiliated when I found out the truth. All those years hiding in fear of a bunch of masquerading Zynots!"

"But . . . what has all that to do with your furnishings?" asked Rowena.

"Gifts," said Azzon. "The Kradens leave gifts of all sorts on their doorsteps. They try to outdo one another, hoping the spirits will be pleased and do them no harm."

"Ahhh!" Darek, Pola, and Rowena laughed.

"You seem fond of the Zynots," said Pola.

Azzon nodded. Then his face grew grave. "We Kradens have been merciless to the Zynots," he

said. "We've killed and maimed them, just for sport, whenever we've caught them down in the foothills.

"They had every right to kill me when they found me. Instead, they brought me to this cave and risked their own lives to care for me. I was so touched by their kindness, I became a changed man."

Darek, Pola, and Rowena had been listening quietly. Now Darek spoke up. "But . . . if you are changed, why won't you help us?" he asked. "Why are you still loyal to your sons?"

Azzon's eyes filled with pain. "I was a cruel father," he said. "I made my sons what they are, and I deserve what has befallen me. I do not blame them. I love them . . . more than ever."

Darek sat thinking, remembering all the problems he had caused *his* father, all the times he had disobeyed. And yet his father had risked everything to follow him into Krad. It was a powerful force—a father's love.

"The love you feel for your sons," Darek said

quietly, "is like the love our fathers feel for us. That's why they followed us here. That's why they are in trouble. Surely you can understand."

Azzon did not answer for a long time. Then he nodded slowly. "I *can* understand," he said. "But that doesn't mean I can help. And even if I could help you rescue them, I couldn't take you back to Zoriac again. I've filled in the tunnel I took you through last time."

"We'll go back the way we came," said Darek.

Azzon shook his head. "You can't," he said. "The dragonsbreath will addle your minds."

"No, it won't," said Darek. He walked over to Zantor and pulled a mask from the saddlebag. "We have these."

Azzon took the mask from Darek's hand. "What is it?" he asked.

"It's a mask that filters out dragonsbreath," Darek told him. "Our ancestors invented them, when they used to fight the Red Fangs."

Azzon stared at the mask in wonderment. "What is it made of?" he asked.

Darek shook his head. "We don't know," he said.

"But I'll bet my father does," Rowena put in. "He's the Chief Elder."

Azzon's brows arched up in surprise. "The Chief Elder of Zoriac is here? In Krad?"

"Yes." Rowena nodded. "He left his throne to come after me. I never dreamed he loved me that much."

The sadness came into Azzon's eyes again. "You are fortunate to have such fathers," he said. "Would that I had been such a father to my sons."

"Perhaps you still can be," said Darek. "It's never too late."

Azzon shook his head. "You don't know my sons," he said. "They were raised on the battlefield. Their lullabies were the screams of dragons in the gaming pits. They would as soon kill me as look at me."

Darek, Pola, and Rowena exchanged sorrowful glances.

"Do not pity me!" Azzon snapped. "I have

made my destiny. I am content to pay the price. My only concern now is, what am I to do with you?"

Zantor was still shuffling around the room, poking his head into this and that, snuffling and sniffling. Now there came a sudden crash and they all jumped.

"*Zatz!*" shouted Azzon. "Look what your beast has done!"

Zantor had upset a shelf high up on the wall. Bottles, jugs, and beakers tumbled to the floor.

"Sorry!" cried Darek. "He didn't mean anything. He was probably just looking for something to eat."

"Dratted dragon!" Azzon shouted. "Those are my potions!" He strode across the room and knelt beside Zantor, trying to salvage what he could. Darek ran over to try and help. Then suddenly he stopped in his tracks. Zantor was shrinking!

"Zantor!" he cried. "What's happening?"

Azzon looked at the dragon. "Oh, he'll be all right," he said shortly. "He must have sampled

the youth potion. It will just make him younger for a while."

"Younger?" cried Darek. "For how long?"

Azzon shrugged. "A day. Maybe two. Depends how much he drank. Unless he gets upset or angry. That could get his blood racing and snap him out of it."

Darek looked at Zantor, who had shrunken down to the size of a newborn. He was sitting quite happily amidst the mess, looking anything but upset. In fact, he had his snout in another beaker!

"Oh no!" cried Darek. "Now what's he got?"

Azzon reached out and snatched the beaker away. He held it up to the light. Then he chuckled. "This one won't hurt him," he said. "But he's going to stink for a while."

9

Darek couldn't sleep. Zantor had insisted on crawling into bed with him, and the smell, like rotten eggs, was making him ill. Not only that. Each time Darek tried to move, little Zantor only snuggled closer. He *was* awfully cute, Darek had to admit, if not for the smell. But Darek hoped Zantor wouldn't stay small for long. They would need him for the rescue, whenever or however *that* happened. One thing was certain. Azzon was not going to help.

Darek felt a tug on his arm.

"Go to back to sleep, Zantor," he mumbled. "I'm here."

There was a little twitter near his ear. "Not Zantor," someone whispered. "Mizzle!"

Darek's eyes flew wide open. "Mizzle!" he whispered. "What are you doing here? You'll get sick."

"Know where fathers are," the small creature whispered.

"What?" Darek sat up.

"Sssss!" said Mizzle, pressing a skinny little finger to his lips. "Need be quiet."

"Why would you help us?" asked Darek. "I thought you were Azzon's friend."

"Mizzle be Azzon's friend," the little creature replied. "But Zooba be Mizzle's father. Ye helped me father. Me help ye father."

Darek smiled and nodded. Zantor poked his head out from under the blankets.

Mizzle looked startled. "Ye dragon?" he questioned.

"Yeah," Darek whispered. "He got into some

of Azzon's potions. Azzon said it will wear off in a day or two."

Mizzle pinched his nose. "Gleep," he said.

Darek nodded. "Yeah. Tell me about it!"

Mizzle giggled again. "Hurry," he said. "Follow."

"Go get Pola and Rowena," Darek told Zantor. "And be quiet about it." Zantor scurried away and Darek pulled his breeches on.

Pola and Rowena came in rubbing their eyes. "What's going on?" they asked.

"Mizzle knows where our fathers are," said Darek. "Grab the masks and let's go."

It was dark and damp and hard to see. The mists swirled as thickly in the valley this night as in the mountains. Mizzle led them carefully past the great cage where the Kradens' fierce Red Fanged dragons slept. Darek shivered, looking at the giant beasts so close on the other side of the fence. One rolled over and belched a stream of fire into the

night and Darek and the others nearly fell over
each other in their haste to get away.

As they drew closer to the village they heard
a fierce din of shrieking and moaning. Darek's
skin prickled. Suddenly a dark shape flew out of
the night, almost bowling them over. It made a

hideous face and waved long, sharp claws. It danced around them for a moment, howling and flailing its claws, then ran off toward the village, cackling wildly.

"What was *that?*" cried Darek.

"Night Spirit," said Mizzle with a giggle.

"Lord," whispered Rowena. "No wonder the Kradens bar their doors."

Up ahead the dark battlements of Castle Krad loomed. Darek's heart beat faster. Night Spirits or no, he didn't like passing so close to that wicked place. Inside its walls lived the evil Zahr. A shift in the wind or a sudden shower and Zahr's men would be free to patrol the streets again.

"I don't like this," Pola whispered.

Darek and Rowena nodded their agreement.

Zantor seemed unconcerned. He frolicked up ahead with Mizzle, while Drizba and Typra brought up the rear.

When they reached Castle Krad, Mizzle suddenly dashed up to the great doors and pounded on them. He lifted his head and gave an ear-splitting shriek. Darek's heart raced. Was Mizzle betraying them?

"Mizzle!" he cried. "What are you doing? Do you want to get us all killed?"

Mizzle rushed back to them, twittering wildly. "Mizzle scare Zahr!" he cried, clapping his little hands. "Mizzle funny."

"Mizzle not funny!" said Darek. "Mizzle foolish!"

Mizzle hung his head. "Mizzle sorry. Mizzle love Spirit Night," he mumbled.

Darek couldn't help smiling. "Mizzle," he said gently. "Our fathers, remember?"

Mizzle looked up and grinned again. "Fathers, yes!" he cried, scampering off again.

They followed Mizzle toward a group of low hills in the distance. As they got closer, Darek could make out a dark opening in the hillside.

Mizzle pointed. "Mines," he said.

"Our fathers are in there?" asked Rowena.

"Men slaves work mines," said Mizzle. He stretched his hand up high. "Big boys too. Small boys work dragons."

"Yes." Darek nodded. He and the others re-membered everything about their slave days now.

They were approaching the opening. A great door stood barred across it.

"Keep out Night Spirits," said Mizzle with a giggle.

"How will *we* get in?" Pola asked.

"Come," said Mizzle. "Be quick." He pointed to the sky. "Daylight come soon. Burn off mist." He scampered up the steep hillside with Zantor close on his heels. Darek followed. He found them at the crest, staring down at a small, square opening.

"What is it?" asked Pola and Rowena as they came up behind.

"Looks like an old air shaft," said Darek. "But it's sealed and there are bars across it."

"I'll get Drizba's tether," Rowena offered. "We can tie one end to the grate and let her pull it free."

"Great idea," said Darek.

Mizzle howled his loudest to cover the noise, and in no time at all the grate was out. The group pried off the lid and knelt around the opening. They could see a light flickering below and hear the murmur of voices.

"Guards," said Mizzle.

"We've got to distract them," said Pola.

"Me get Zynots," said Mizzle. "Make much noise."

68

"That'll help," said Darek, "but we've got to get them out of that room down there somehow." He lifted his mask to scratch his nose and Zantor's stench nearly made him gag.

"Zatz, Zantor, you stink!" he whispered.

"That's it!" cried Pola.

"What's it?" asked Darek.

"You'll see," said Pola. "Rowena, get Drizba's tether again."

10

Zantor dangled from the end of the tether, inside the shaft, just above the guard's room. He stared up at Darek, Pola, and Rowena with mournful eyes.

"Shush," Darek begged him, pressing a finger to his lips. "Don't make a sound, okay?"

Rrronk, came a loud and clear mind message.

Darek smiled. "It shouldn't be much longer," he whispered.

Sure enough, a moment later he heard one of the guards say, "Phew! What *is* that smell?"

"I don't know," another one replied. "Zatz! It smells like something died!"

"Aargh! I can't take it," a third put in. "I've got to get out of here."

There was a murmur of agreement, a scraping of chairs, and then silence. Darek grinned down at Zantor. "Good job!" he whispered.

Thrummm, came the soft reply.

"EEEyiiiooowwll!! Arrooogh!! Grraahrr!!" Mizzle was back with his friends and they were setting up a mighty din.

"Let's go," whispered Darek.

Slowly they lowered Zantor to the floor of the room, then one by one they slid down the rope to join him. Darek untied Zantor, who greedily attacked a bowl of fruit on the guard's table.

"Little guy's hungry," whispered Pola. "Come to think of it, so am I."

"Forget it, Pola," said Darek. "We've got more to worry about than our stomachs." He pushed his mask back and looked around. One tunnel led upward away from the room, and another down.

"Which way?" he whispered.

"My guess would be down," said Rowena.

Pola nodded. "Mine too."

"All right," said Darek. "Let's go." He grabbed a torch from the wall and led the way into the tunnel.

"Hey," cried Rowena. "Look what *I* found." She reached up high on the wall and took down a heavy ring of keys.

Darek and Pola grinned. "This is almost too easy," said Pola.

"Don't count your zoks before they hatch," Darek warned.

The tunnel was narrow and dank. Water oozed out of the walls and the floor was slimy with mold. The deeper they went, the colder it became.

Darek shivered. "I hate to think of our fathers living down here," he said.

"Or the other Zorian slaves," said Rowena quietly.

Darek swallowed. That *was* hard to think about. Just as it was difficult to think about Arnod and the other slave friends they had left behind on their last visit to Krad. They had promised to return and help those friends one day.

"Someday, somehow, we'll help them all," he whispered. "But right now we've only got enough masks to get our fathers and Clep back through the mountains."

Pola and Rowena nodded in sad agreement.

"Listen!" Pola suddenly whispered.

They froze. Heavy footsteps were coming up the tunnel toward them. Darek looked around wildly, then remembered a small niche in the wall a short way back.

"Hurry!" he cried, dousing his torch.

The three ran back and crowded into the niche. Then they pulled Zantor in behind them, pinching their noses at his stench. Their hearts pounded as the steps came closer. Torchlight flickered farther down in the tunnel and then two guards came into view. Darek held his breath and tried to shrink further into the shadows as they clomped

by. Just then, Zantor let out a small belch. Darek's
heart lurched.

"What was that?" one of the guards asked.

"What?" asked the other. "I didn't hear anything."

"Ugh! What's that smell?" the first guard cried.
Then, "Zatz, man! Is that you! What in Krad did
you eat for dinner?!"

"It's not me," the second man cried. "It must
be *you*, you sloth!"

Darek, Pola, and Rowena clapped their hands over their mouths to keep from laughing. They could still hear the two men arguing as their footsteps faded away.

"Phew," whispered Rowena, "that was close."

"Yeah." Pola nodded. "And now we've lost our light."

"Oh, no we haven't," said Darek. "You forget the many talents of our smelly little friend here." He lifted the torch. "Zantor," he said, "light, please."

11

Darek lifted his torch high and peered in through the small barred window of the cell door. Then he shook his head. "Not them," he whispered. He and the others were growing discouraged. They'd peeked into dozens of cells but had yet to find Clep or any of their fathers among the sleeping slaves.

"It'll be dawn soon," said Rowena. "We're running out of time."

"We'd better get back," said Pola. "It won't help anything if we're captured."

Pola was right, Darek realized, but . . . they

were so close! "Just a few more cells," he said. "Then we'll go." He crept up to the next door and peered in, then the next, then his mouth dropped open. "It's them!" he cried.

Pola and Rowena scrambled to get a peek.

"Praise Lord Eternal," Rowena whispered, tears filling her eyes.

"Try the keys," cried Darek. "Hurry!"

Rowena took out her keys and fumbled with the lock. Several didn't work, and then one turned and the door swung open.

"Thrummm," sang Zantor. He flew by and leapt joyfully on Darek's sleeping brother.

"What the—"

"Shush!" cried Darek. He crouched at his brother's side. "Quiet, Clep. We've come to rescue you."

Clep's eyes grew wide. "Darek!" They grabbed each other in a rough hug. "Lord Eternal! I thought I'd never see you again!"

The fathers were carefully wakened as well, and after a quick round of hugs and tears, Darek pressed them to get going.

"Who's the little dragon?" his father asked. "And why does he smell so bad?"

"It's Zantor," said Darek with a soft laugh. "I'll explain later. If we don't get out of here before the sun comes up, the Kradens will be able to follow us. Hurry!"

"What of the other slaves?" asked the Chief Elder.

"We have no way of getting them through the mountains," said Darek. "If we free them now, they'll only perish."

The Chief Elder hesitated. "But they are Zorians, like us," he said. "They are our friends."

"Yes." Rowena took her father's hand. "And that is why we must escape while we can. So that one day we can return and help them."

The Chief Elder nodded. "Onward then," he said.

Darek led the way back, but as they approached the guards' room once again they heard a din of excited voices. Someone was shouting orders to search the tunnels! They had been discovered.

"This way," said Darek's father, hurrying to the front of the group. "We'll have to make a run for the main entrance." He led the way down another passage and Darek followed willingly. It felt good, for the moment, to be a kid again, to let his father take control.

The passage twisted this way and that. Soon they heard shouts and pounding footsteps behind them.

"Run faster!" came Clep's voice from behind.

Darek's breath was already coming in ragged puffs, but he pushed himself even harder. Pola and Rowena were close on his heels, and Zantor fluttered overhead. Clep and the other fathers brought up the rear. At last the tunnel began to widen. Darek could hear the howling of Mizzle and his Night Spirits in the distance.

"We must be near the entrance," Darek cried over his shoulder.

Sure enough, they rounded a bend and there stood the huge wooden doors. The way to freedom!

Then Darek's father stepped aside and Darek saw that between them and the doors stood a dozen armed guards.

12

Darek tried to turn back, but it was too late. More guards were already herding Pola, Rowena, and the others into the center of the room. They all huddled together, downcast, and breathing heavily. Zantor seemed to sense Darek's despair.

"*Rrronk*," he cried softly.

"Well, well," said one of the guards. "What have we here? A family reunion? How cozy."

Outside, Darek could hear Mizzle and the others still howling and shrieking. He swallowed hard and looked down. They had come so close to free-dom. *So close!* Tears stung his eyes.

One of the guards stepped forward. "I know these three," he said. "These are the three whelps that escaped from the dragon nurseries a while back."

Darek looked up—into the eyes of Daxon, Master of the stockyards. Daxon's eyes narrowed.

"That's right, boy," Daxon said. "It's me. Your old Master. Thanks to you I've been demoted to mine guard." He laughed wickedly. "Now I'll have a chance to redeem myself."

Daxon stepped forward and grabbed Darek by the shoulders and started to shake him. Out of the corner of his eye, Darek saw his father rush forward. But another guard shoved him aside.

"Rrronk, rrronk!" cried Zantor. He flew up and clawed at Daxon, but Daxon brushed him off like a flea. "Kill that dragonling!" he bellowed to the other guards.

"Rrronk, rrronk!" Darek heard Zantor cry as several guards grabbed for him.

"No!" Darek shouted. "Please!" But then a

powerful blow stung him across the cheek. He tasted blood in his mouth.

"*Rrronk, rrrOWK, GRRAWWWK!*" Darek heard. Then suddenly there came a great thrashing and crashing. Guards went flying and a burst of flame flashed above Darek's head, scorching Daxon's beard.

"Aagh!" Daxon cried. He let go of Darek and began to beat at the flames.

Darek turned. Zantor was full size again, and angrier than Darek had ever seen him! Guards flew left and right. Weapons clattered to the floor. Bursts of flame flashed around the room like lightning. With cries of terror the guards gathered up their fallen comrades and ran for the tunnel.

"Zantor!" Darek cried. "The doors! Hurry!"

With a scream of fury, Zantor turned and hurled himself at the heavy doors. They splintered like tinder, spilling him out into the night.

"C'mon!" Darek motioned to the others. "Follow me!"

Out they rushed, one and all, into the waiting arms of the Night Spirits.

13

Darek, Pola, and Rowena stood beside their dragons. Their fathers were at their shoulders, and Clep at Darek's side. Darek couldn't see the others' faces behind their battle masks, but their eyes danced with joy. Even the Black Mountains seemed cheerful today.

"Well," said Darek's father proudly. "It seems that you've proven yourself a hero once again, my son."

Darek blushed and glanced at the throng of Zynots who had come to say good-bye. "I'm not the hero, Father," he said. He stroked Zantor's neck and looked up at Mizzle, who sat perched on the dragon's head. "These two are the heroes."

Zantor *thrumm*ed softly, and Mizzle twittered.

Zooba grinned. "Come ye down here, son," he called.

Mizzle slid down Zantor's back into his father's arms. Darek removed his mask for a moment and reached a hand out to the little Zynot. "How can I ever thank you, my friend?" he asked.

Mizzle grinned. "No need thank Mizzle," he said. "Mizzle be glad ye be with ye fathers. All be happy now, like Mizzle and Zooba." He smiled up into his own father's eyes.

"Yes." Darek glanced at Clep and his father. They *would* be happy now. They were on their way home. Home to Zoriac, the farm, and Mother. All would be happy. All except the slaves they were once again leaving behind. And Azzon. For a moment Darek's mood darkened. He silently re-newed his vow to fulfill his promise to the slaves one day. That was all he could do just now. And as for Azzon . . . Suddenly Darek had a thought.

"Rowena," he cried. "Do we still have that spare mask?"

Rowena nodded. "Yes," she said. "It's in Drizba's saddle bag."

"Can you toss it to me?" asked Darek.

Rowena shrugged and pulled out the mask. She tossed it to Darek, who caught it and handed it to Mizzle.

"Azzon may not be able to be with his sons," Darek said. "But at least he can be with his friends. With this on he can spend as much time up here with you as he likes."

Mizzle took the mask, put it on, and started dancing around. "Azzon be glad," he cried. "Zynots be glad, too."

He looked so comical in the oversized mask that Darek and the others couldn't help laughing.

"Good-bye, little Night Spirit," said Darek with a wink.

"*Grraahrr!*" cried Mizzle, flailing his arms.

Then he took off the mask and raised his hand
in farewell. " 'Bye, Dragon Boy. Come ye back
some day!"

Darek nodded, then climbed into his saddle and
helped his father and Clep up behind him.

"Home, Zantor," he said softly.

Thrummm, sang the dragon. *Thrummm,*
thrummm, thrummm.

About the Author

Jackie French Koller is the award-winning author of nearly twenty books for children and young adults. She started the *Dragonling* series at the request of her youngest son, Devin, then in the third grade, because dragons were his "second favorite animals—next to dogs."

The Dragonling

Join Darek and his dragonling friend Zantor
for fun and adventure.

"The characters are believable, and their adventures,
fears, and suspicions make for exciting reading
for children moving into chapter books."

—*School Library Journal*

o **A Dragon in the Family** 89786-1/$3.50
o **The Dragonling** 86790-3/$3.50
o **Dragon Quest** 00193-0/$3.50
o **Dragons of Krad** 00194-9/$3.50
o **Dragon Trouble** 01399-8/$3.50

Don't miss the next exciting adventure!
By Jackie French Koller

 A MINSTREL® BOOK

Published by Pocket Books

Simon & Schuster Mail Order Dept. BWB
200 Old Tappan Rd., Old Tappan, N.J. 07675

Please send me the books I have checked above. I am enclosing $_____ (please add $0.75 to cover the postage and handling for each order. Please add appropriate sales tax). Send check or money order--no cash or C.O.D.'s please. Allow up to six weeks for delivery. For purchase over $10.00 you may use VISA: card number, expiration date and customer signature must be included.

Name _____

Address _____

City _____ State/Zip _____

VISA Card # _____ Exp.Date _____

Signature _____

1290-02

BRAND-NEW SERIES!

Meet up with suspense and mystery in

#1 The Gross Ghost Mystery

Frank and Joe are making friends and meeting monsters!

#2 The Karate Clue

Somebody's kicking up a major mess!

#3 First Day, Worst Day

Everybody's mad at Joe! Is he a tattletale?

By Franklin W. Dixon

Look for a brand-new story every other month
at your local bookseller

 A MINSTREL® BOOK

Published by Pocket Books

1398-01